To Sinan, Erol, and Semih. Love you to the
Ramadan Moon and back.
—M.O.Y.

To Michelle and Khaled, with lots of love,
for all the special Ramadans we've shared
and will continue to share together.
—H.A.

Acknowledgments:
My heartfelt gratitude to Renée LaTulippe, Imam Khalid Latif, the
Highlights Foundation, Megan Ilnitzki, and the Harper team for
their valuable guidance, encouragement, and support.
—M.O.Y.

Ramadan Kareem
Text copyright © 2024 by M. O. Yuksel
Illustrations copyright © 2024 by Hatem Aly
All rights reserved. Manufactured in Italy.

Library of Congress Control Number: 2023937104
ISBN 978-0-06-324012-4

The artist used digital rendering on Adobe Photoshop along with scans of
ink washes, textures, and patterns to create the artwork for this book.
Typography by Rachel Zegar
23 24 25 26 27 RTLO 10 9 8 7 6 5 4 3 2 1

First Edition

Ramadan Kareem

Written by M. O. Yuksel ◆ Illustrated by Hatem Aly

HARPER

We gather
to gaze at the new crescent moon.
Ramadan Kareem!
The holy month of mercy
and blessings has begun.

It's my favorite time of the year—
Ramadan is here!
Hooray!
This time, Mom says
I can practice fasting.

The drummer beats her drum—
doum, da, doum-doum!—
waking us for suhoor,
the predawn meal.

Eggs sizzle,
toasters pop,
qatayefs flip.

I rub my sleepy eyes and drift
toward the most delicious smell—
tasty, juicy kofta.

My teita's eyes twinkle—
I know she's proud of me for waking up
early for suhoor.
It's so early, the sun is still sleeping.

The calls to prayer from mosques
echo in the air.
We stand together in devotion.
After salah, we dash off
to open shops,
to go to school,
to meet friends.
"Ramadan Mubarak!" we say.

Ba-boom, ba-boom, ba-boom!
My heart thumps.
I can't wait to tell my friends
I'm fasting for the first time.
I will be extra kind, caring, and polite.

And if anyone argues with me,
I will say,
"I'm fasting. I'm fasting."

"Hot, fresh roti!" a woman calls.
"Sweet, ripe watermelons!" a man hollers.

In the hustle and bustle of the bazaar,
we pick the best and freshest ones
in preparation for iftar, the fast-breaking meal.

Clink,
clink,
clink!

The man in the wheelchair selling tissues
smiles bright like sunshine
when I donate my coins.
My heart smiles back.

Bismillahi'r-rahmani'r-rahim.
We pray because the prayer
of a fasting person
is always accepted.

I trace the lines of the Qur'an on my abuela's lap,
which feels warm and cozy
like a soft blanket.

She tells me the Qur'an was revealed
to us during Ramadan.
Iqra—read—*was the first word.*

Knead, fold, chop, sizzle, steam!

We prepare iftar with extra
care and love—
feeding a fasting person brings
immense blessings.

Ideas bubble in my head
like the stew my dad is making.
I glue sparkles on my Ramadan cards,
and . . .

Knock, knock, knock!
. . . go door to door
giving neighbors gifts and spreading
good cheer!
Ramadan Kareem!

Trains, buses, and cars
whoosh by!

We rush home
as shadows grow long
in the late afternoon sun.

I slouch in front of the clock that

tick,
   tick,
      ticks

the time along
like a tired turtle.
"Iftar will never come!"

Dad tells me time will pass
more quickly
if we help others.
Dad and I pack donations
for our local shelter.

As-salaamu Alaykum!
We visit family and friends,
bringing delicious dishes to share.
Our blessings are multiplied.

My cousins and friends help set the table.
Plates of yummy samosas stream in.

I sway to the sweet smells swirling through the air.
My mouth waters—
"Is it iftar time yet?!"

Our palms open in prayer,
we pray our fast and good deeds are accepted,
we pray for the poor and less fortunate,
we pray for peace, love, and harmony.

Iftar is finally here!
I try to say a prayer,
but my tummy won't stop rumbling and grumbling—
roar, roar, ROAR!

My throat scratches like sandpaper.
I understand
the many people around the world,
like me,
who hunger and thirst.

Sweet, plump dates fill our mouths
as we break our fast.
Cool, refreshing water
soothes our throats.

Yum, yum, yum!
*Everything tastes sweeter than sweet,
even the kimchi!*

*I hold my head up high.
I knew I could fast all day
and I proved it . . .
especially to my older brother,
who bet I couldn't do it.*

We pause our feast to pray
together in gratitude
for all our blessings.

I sprint back to the table
and gobble up the rest of my iftar
until my tummy is full.

Ahhhhhhhhh!
Alhamdulillah.
That was worth
waiting for.

Yearning for the Night of Power,
which is better than a thousand nights,
we pray longingly,
we give generously,
we reflect mindfully.

I play with my friends
at the masjid during tarawih.
We try to listen
to the imam recite the Qur'an,
but sometimes
tickles and giggles
ERUPT!

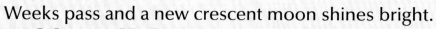

Weeks pass and a new crescent moon shines bright.
Subhanallah!
We've fasted a whole month.

Zakat money, new outfits,
gifts, sweets, and treats
are ready to welcome
our joyful holiday, **Eid al-Fitr**.

I twirl round and round
  like a whirling dervish
    and cheer at the sight of
      twinkly lights,
        crescent moons,
          and balloons
            my dadajon and I hung.

I sing at the top of my lungs—
**tomorrow is going to be
so much fun!**

We will miss Ramadan
and can't wait until next year,
when the month of mercy and blessings
is upon us once more.

Ramadan was great!
Now it's time to celebrate!
After Eid prayer,
my aunties and uncles give me
eidi and gifts.
Hooray!

Oh, how I love Ramadan!

Eid Mubarak!

WHAT IS RAMADAN?

Ramadan is celebrated worldwide by Muslims, people who practice the religion of Islam. It is a time of increased devotion, prayer, charity, self-reflection, and fasting.

Ramadan is the ninth month of the Islamic calendar. The Islamic calendar is based on a lunar cycle and is eleven days shorter than the solar or Gregorian calendar. This is why Ramadan shifts about eleven days earlier each year on the Gregorian calendar.

Traditionally, Muslims mark the beginning of Ramadan by looking at the night sky for the new crescent moon. This is the method that was followed by the Prophet Muhammad. Similarly, some Muslims still prefer to follow the traditional method while others rely on modern technology to determine the beginning of Ramadan.

During this month, Muslims engage in a variety of religious, charitable, and communal activities, and fast every day by not eating or drinking anything from just before sunrise until sunset. Muslims are required to fast during Ramadan once they reach puberty, except those who are sick, traveling, elderly, pregnant, breastfeeding, or menstruating. Children are not required to fast, although some may voluntarily fast for half or full days as practice for later in life.

The holiday Eid al-Fitr is celebrated at the end of Ramadan in various ways by different cultures across the globe. But in general, families go to the mosque for Eid prayer and then gather with family and friends.

For more information about Ramadan and fun craft activities, please visit moyuksel.com.

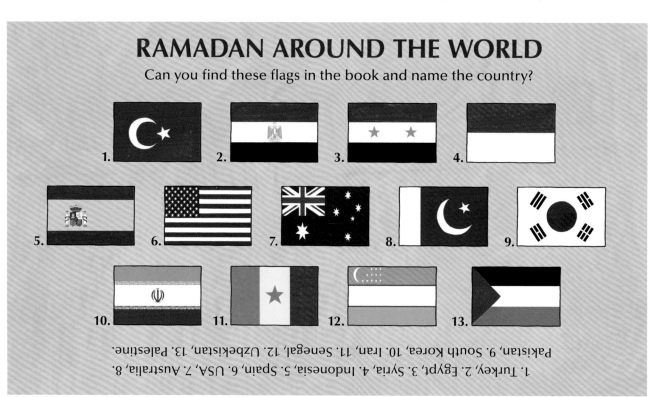

RAMADAN AROUND THE WORLD
Can you find these flags in the book and name the country?

1. Turkey, 2. Egypt, 3. Syria, 4. Indonesia, 5. Spain, 6. USA, 7. Australia, 8. Pakistan, 9. South Korea, 10. Iran, 11. Senegal, 12. Uzbekistan, 13. Palestine.

GLOSSARY

Abuela (AH-bweh-la): Grandmother

Alhamdulillah (AL-Ham-Du-lil-LAH): All praise is due to God

Baba (BA-BA): Father

Bazaar (buh-zahr): Marketplace

Bismillahi'r-rahmani'r-rahim (BIS-mil-LA-hir RAH-MAA-nir RA-heem): In the name of God, the Most Gracious, the Most Merciful

Dadajon (DA-DA-jon): Father; mainly used in the Uzbek language

Dervish (DAR-vish): Member of a Muslim Sufi religious order

Eid (EED): Celebration, holiday

Eid al-Fitr (EED ul-Fit-ur): Festival of Breaking the Fast; a three-day holiday celebrated at the end of Ramadan

Eid Mubarak (EED MU-ba-ruck): Happy or blessed holiday

Eidi (EE-DEE): Money given to children on Eid

Iftar (If-taar): The fast-breaking meal after sunset

Imam (E-maam): A teacher or person who leads prayer

Iqra (Iq-raw): Read or recite

Islam (is-lAm): An Abrahamic monotheistic religion that Muslims follow. It means complete, voluntary submission to God

Kareem (KA-reem): Generous; when used after the word Ramadan, it means blessings and greetings

Kimchi (kim-chi): Korean fermented cabbage that is often spicy

Kofta (kaf-ta): Meatballs made with minced meat and spices

Mosque (mAosk): A place of worship for Muslims. Also referred to as masjid or jamii

Night of Power: The night the first verses of the Qur'an were revealed. Also referred to as Lailat al-Qadr

Qatayef (Ka-Ta-yef): Stuffed pancakes popular in Egypt and other Arabic countries

Qur'an (QUR-ann): The holy book of Islam

Roti (row-ti): Bread

Salah (Sa-LAh): Prayers performed by Muslims. Also known as namaz or salat

Samosa (SA-MO-SA): South Asian pastry filled with minced meat or vegetables

Subhanallah (sub-HAN-AL-LAWH): Glory be to God

Suhoor (Su-Hoor): The predawn meal before the start of the fasting day during Ramadan. Also spelled as suhur or sahur

Tarawih (Ta-Ra-Weeh): Extra voluntary nightly prayers during Ramadan

Teita (Tay-tah): Grandmother; used in some Arabic-speaking countries such as Egypt and Lebanon

Zakat (Za-kat): Charity money each Muslim is expected to give once a year

ADDITIONAL RESOURCES

Heiligman, Deborah. *Celebrate Ramadan & Eid Al-Fitr*. National Geographic Books, 2006.

Khan, Ausma Zehanat. *Ramadan: The Holy Month of Fasting*. Orca Publishing, 2018.

MacMillan, Dianne M. *Ramadan and Id al-Fitr*. Enslow, 2008.